Love
Is
Powerful

Love
Is
Powerful

Heather Dean Brewer

illustrated by
LeUyen Pham

WALKER BOOKS
AND SUBSIDIARIES
LONDON · BOSTON · SYDNEY · AUCKLAND

Mari spilled her crayons onto the table. They made a messy rainbow.

"What are we colouring, Mama?" she asked.

Mama smiled. "A message for the world."

Mari ran to the window and pressed her nose to the glass. Far below, people walked in different directions. Buses, cars and taxis honked and grumbled down the busy street.

Mari asked, "How will the whole world hear?"

"They'll hear," Mama said, "because love is powerful."

Mari climbed onto her mama's lap. The crayons smelled sharp and new. Mama used one to write some letters. Even though Mama's words stretched across the poster, they would be too small for the world to read, Mari thought.

Mari picked up a crayon. As she made her own sign, she imagined her friends in their homes across the city,

Grandma and Grampa a plane ride away, and all the people in other countries.

Mari wondered, "How will the whole world see our message?"

Mama hugged her close. "They'll see," she said, "because love is powerful."

Mama handed her a
coat, and then they
both laced up their
shoes. Mari tucked the
posters under one arm
and held Mama's hand
with the other.

They slipped through
the lift doors.

Down,

down,

down

they went,

all the way to the hallway.

Mari hopped onto the pavement, then stopped and looked up. The street was packed with people – more people than she'd ever seen in her entire life. Mari tugged on Mama's arm to ask her to kneel down. Then she whispered in Mama's ear,

"Mama, it's so loud, and there's so many people. They won't hear our message."

Mama said, "They will, little Mari."

WE MAY NOT HAVE CHOSEN THE TIME. BUT THE TIME HAS CHOSEN US."

- John Lewis

RESPECT

BE KIND

Love is powerful

Mama lifted Mari up, and for a moment she felt like she was flying. On top of Mama's shoulders, Mari could see the crowd swell for blocks – hundreds and thousands, even hundreds of thousands, of people marching down the street.

Some held signs like Mari's, all saying different things. Everyone cheered as they walked together. Mama joined them. Mari bobbed above the crowd like a canary fluttering over trees. She felt as tall as one of the buildings.

HATE CANNOT DRIVE OUT HATE. ONLY LOVE CAN

Mari raised her sign for everyone to see. Even though she was small and the crowd very big, so big she didn't think anyone would hear, she called out her message.

Through the roar, her voice was heard and someone shouted the message back. Mari yelled again, and more joined in. Again she yelled the message.

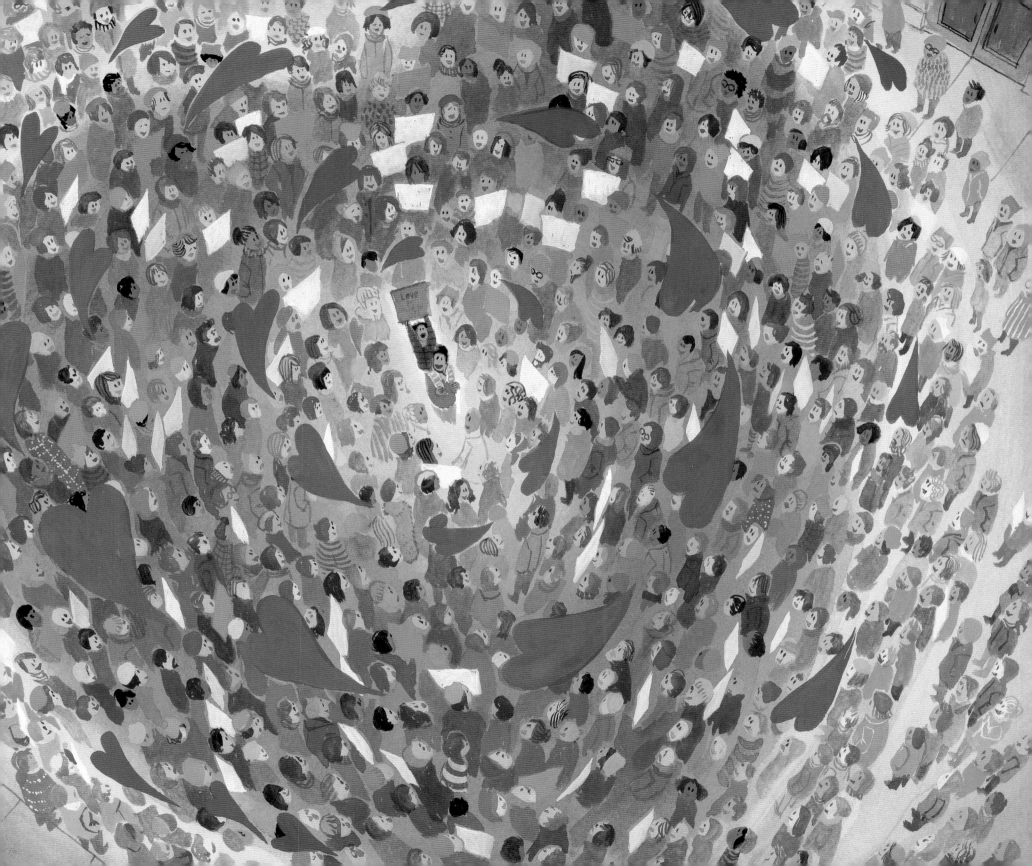

This time, when the crowd called back, Mari's message rumbled down the street and echoed off the buildings. It was as loud as breaking waves.

"Love is

A NOTE FROM MARI

I was only six years old, but I knew why we were there. Our new president had said some terrible things about women. He made people feel scared and angry. We went to the Women's March, along with hundreds of thousands of people, that cold day to show that love really is powerful!

A few of my friends were with me with their parents – we rode the subway from Harlem to Midtown together after spending time making our signs. I made two: "Love Is Powerful" and "Be Kind". When we joined the crowd at the march, I couldn't see that well and was tired of walking. My mom lifted me up onto her shoulders as we marched down the crowded streets.

When I sat on my mom's shoulders, I felt proud holding the signs I had made earlier that day. When I called out "Love is powerful", to my surprise, the people close to me repeated it back. Each time I said it, more people joined in. Soon hundreds of people were echoing my chant of "Love is powerful!" At that moment, I really felt its power! One voice can be heard, and one voice can make a difference. My advice to you is: believe in yourself, be confident, and don't be afraid to speak up. And remember to speak up not just for yourself, but for other people, too.

Love, Mari

For You:
Be brave, be loud, stick together, and go change the world.
And for my mom and dad,
who helped the quietest girl in school find her voice.
HDB

To Mom and Dad.

LP

First published 2020 by Walker Books Ltd
87 Vauxhall Walk, London SE11 5HJ

2 4 6 8 10 9 7 5 3 1

Text © 2020 by Heather Dean Brewer
Illustrations © 2020 by LeUyen Pham
Photograph of Mari © 2017 by Claire Callagy
Used by permission of the photographer.

The right of Heather Dean Brewer and LeUyen Pham to be identified as author and illustrator
respectively of this work has been asserted by them in accordance with
the Copyright, Designs and Patents Act 1988

This book has been typeset in ITC Officina Sans

Printed in China

British Library Cataloguing in Publication Data:
a catalogue record for this book is available from the British Library

ISBN 978-1-4063-9743-7

www.walker.co.uk